Andrew Draws

David McPhail

Holiday House / New York

HOLIDAY HOUSE is registered in the U.S. Patent and Trademark Office.
Printed and Bound in April 2014 at Toppan Leefung, DongGuan City, China.
The artwork was drawn with Liquitex burnt umber ink,
using a crowquill pen on Strathmore 500 series 3-ply smooth paper,
then colored with Winsor & Newton watercolors.
The sketches on the endpapers
are from the artist's original sketch dummy.
www.holidayhouse.com
First Edition
1 3 5 7 9 10 8 6 4 2

Library of Congress Cataloging-in-Publication Data
McPhail, David, 1940- author, illustrator.
Andrew draws / by David McPhail. — First edition.
pages cm
ISBN 978-0-8234-3063-5 (hardcover)
[1. Drawing—Fiction.] I. Title.
PZ7.M478818Am 2014
[Fic]—dc23
2013037251

To
Julian

Andrew found a crayon under the sofa.

He picked it up and began to
make scribbles on the floor.

"Stop!" said his mother.

Andrew's grandmother came to the rescue. She gave him a pad of paper to draw on.

After that Andrew drew . . .

and drew.

At first it was hard to tell what Andrew
had drawn.

"What a pretty flower!" his mother said.

"It's a dog," said Andrew.

But Andrew kept at it.

Andrew
drew just
about
anywhere.

He drew
animals at
the zoo.

He drew fish and penguins at the aquarium.

And at the art museum Andrew
copied the paintings he liked most.

One day Andrew drew a picture of
a bird and gave it to his grandmother.
The bird flew right off the page and
landed on her shoulder.

"Oh my," she said.

Then Andrew drew a cat for his mother.
"Thank you," she said. "I've always
wanted a cat!"

Andrew drew a big, soft chair for his father.
"I like it," said his father. "It's very comfortable."

Word of Andrew's amazing ability spread. Even the president heard about it.

He called Andrew on the telephone.

"There are many problems in the world," said the president. "Perhaps you can help fix them."

Andrew agreed to try.
He drew a picture of some trucks
filled with food for hungry people . . .

and one of a big ship loaded with supplies for people whose homes had been washed away by a flood.

He drew pictures of schools and
hospitals and sent them where they
were needed.

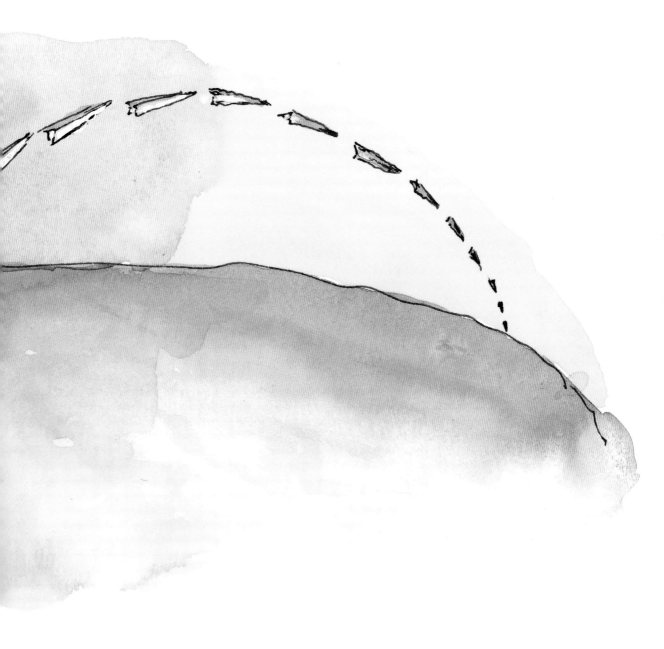

Andrew drew
so many pictures
that his crayon
wore down to
a stub, and his
paper was nearly
used up.

With his last bit of crayon and his
final sheet of paper, Andrew made a
drawing for himself.

Also by David McPhail

Bad Dog

Boy, Bird, and Dog

Sick Day